BELINDA'S HURRICANE

Belinda's always sad when the end of August comes and
it's time to leave her granny's house on the island.
But this year on Belinda's last day, she learns that
a hurricane's coming—which means she and Granny May
will have to stay put.

Safe and dry from the storm, snuggled up listening to Granny's
stories, Belinda doesn't expect the visitor who comes
knocking at their door—or that she'll need all her courage when
she has to attempt a daring rescue...

"Winthrop's story is like a well-built play house: solidly constructed,
details suggested but not overelaborated, and everything perfectly in
scale....Well-written books that fall between easy readers and full-
length novels are always welcome. Winthrop has turned the limitations
of the form into virtues."–ALA *Booklist*

BELINDA'S HURRICANE

by Elizabeth Winthrop

pictures by Wendy Watson

Puffin Books

PUFFIN BOOKS

Published by the Penguin Group

Penguin Books USA Inc., 375 Hudson Street, New York, New York 10014, U.S.A.

Penguin Books Ltd, 27 Wrights Lane, London W8 5TZ, England

Penguin Books Australia Ltd, Ringwood, Victoria, Australia

Penguin Books Canada Ltd, 10 Alcorn Avenue, Toronto, Ontario, Canada M4V 3B2

Penguin Books (N.Z.) Ltd, 182–190 Wairau Road, Auckland 10, New Zealand

Penguin Books Ltd, Registered Offices: Harmondsworth, Middlesex, England

First published in the United States of America by E.P. Dutton,
a division of NAL Penguin Inc. 1984
Published in Puffin Books 1989
3   5   7   9   10   8   6   4   2
Text copyright © Elizabeth Winthrop Mahony, 1984
Illustrations copyright © Wendy Watson, 1984
All rights reserved

Winthrop, Elizabeth.   Belinda's hurricane.
Reprint. Originally published: New York: Dutton, 1984.
Summary: While waiting out a fierce hurricane in
her grandmother's house on Fox Island, Belinda has a
chance to get to know her grandmother's reclusive
neighbor, Mr. Fletcher.
[1. Hurricanes—Fiction.   2. Islands—Fiction.
3. Grandmothers—Fiction.   4. Interpersonal relations—
Fiction]   I. Watson, Wendy, ill.   II. Title.
PZ7.W768Bel   1989   [Fic]   88-30686
ISBN 0-14-032985-4

Printed in the United States of America
by R.R. Donnelley & Sons Company, Harrisonburg, VA
Set in Goudy Old Style

for Elizabeth Winthrop Alsop
who stole my name and my heart
at the same time

Contents

Seashells

Belinda and Granny May were sitting on the front porch. They were sorting the seashells that Belinda had collected during her visit.

"I wish I could take them all," Belinda said. "You won't throw any of them out, will you?"

Granny May looked up and smiled. "Of course not, Belinda. I'll put them right upstairs in the same chest with the others. Look, here's a perfect jackknife clam. You can't leave that behind." Granny May dropped it into the "take home" shoe box.

"I wish I didn't have to go," Belinda said. She looked out over the water.

"That's your second wish in five minutes," Granny May said. She sighed. "I wish you didn't have to go either. The house always feels funny without you. It echoes."

For the last three years, ever since she was six, Belinda had come to visit Granny May on Fox Island for the month of August. Her friends from school felt sorry for her. "Poor Belinda," they said. "Too bad you can't come to camp with us. I'm glad I don't have to go visit my grandmother."

But Belinda loved Granny May. They fit together like the two old armchairs that sat on either side of her fireplace. They collected shells and glued them onto little boxes. They picked blueberries and made jam. They got up early in the morning to go fishing in the yellow rowboat. They went to bed late after a big bowl of ice cream with fudge sauce and a game of Parcheesi. Every clear night, they slept with their windows open, so the gulls would wake them up again in the morning.

"Look at the boats. I wonder why they're all coming in so early," Granny May said, staring out at the harbor.

"Now, I'm all done," said Belinda. She tied a string around the shoe box that was filled with shells to take home. "I'm going next door to Mr. Fletcher's, and then I'm going into town. Do you need anything?"

"We're all out of fudge sauce," Granny May said with a grin.

Good-bye Fishface!

Belinda always took one last trip into town to say good-bye to her friends and all the places that she would not see for another year. Today she had to mow Mr. Fletcher's lawn for the last time and collect the money he owed her. Then she would have enough to buy Granny May's birthday present while she was in town.

She had seen the necklace in Miss Lizzie's gift shop her first day on the island. It was a delicate gold necklace with five scallop shells hanging down from it. Each shell was edged in gold. It was the perfect present for Granny May, who loved shells as much as Belinda did, and who loved scallop shells best of all. But the necklace was expensive, and it had taken Belinda a whole month to save up enough money for it.

She had worked down at the fish market, cleaning fish for Joe Smithers. She had fed old Mrs. Greenstone's cat when she went away for a week. But Mr. Fletcher's lawn had been the worst job of all.

Mr. Fletcher was a retired fisherman who lived next door to Granny May. He kept very much to himself. The shades in his house were always pulled way down, and in the three years Belinda had been coming to stay with Granny May, she had barely seen Mr. Fletcher—until this year.

She rounded the corner and was stopped short by a low growl coming from under Mr. Fletcher's porch.

"Oh be quiet, Fishface," she said in as firm a voice as she could muster. But the growling grew louder, and the old bulldog began to crawl out towards her. She ran for the porch steps just as the snarling turned to short, ugly barks and he rushed at her. He was snapped back by the leash just in time and, as usual, she arrived at Mr. Fletcher's door, gasping and furious.

When Mr. Fletcher opened his door, she exploded. "If I didn't need the money so badly, I would never come back here. That dog should be arrested."

He looked at her as if she had just arrived on his porch from outer space. "Nobody else has trouble with him," he said.

"Could you please take him inside today?" Belinda asked, a little calmer.

"He likes it outside," Mr. Fletcher said. "But maybe the lawn doesn't need any mowing today. It's the end of the season."

"Oh no, that's all right, I'll do it," Belinda said quickly. "But if you could give me the money now, then I'll leave the key to the toolshed on that nail above the garage door, and I won't have to come past him again."

He was turning that proposal over in his mind while he dug in the pocket of his baggy pants for the key. "Well, all right," he said. "But you do a good job on that lawn, miss. No skipping the corners just because it's your last time."

"Mr. Fletcher, I am not a corner skipper," Belinda said, drawing herself up as tall as she could. "You should know that by now. I've worked for you a whole month."

He turned back into the house to get the money, shutting the door behind him as usual. What is he trying to hide from me? Belinda wondered as she leaned against the porch rail and waited. Fishface stood at the bottom of the steps, leering up at her just as if he had chased a squirrel up a tree and he knew it had nowhere to come but down. Finally, Mr. Fletcher returned. He handed her the crumpled dollar bills and the key.

"Well, good-bye Mr. Fletcher," she said cheerily. "See you next summer."

"Maybe," he said. "Watch those corners."

6

"Good-bye Fishface," she called over the porch railing as she went around to the back stairs.

She could hear him barking in frustration the whole time she mowed the lawn.

The Necklace

Her first stop in town was always the fishing dock.

"Hi there Belinda," a voice called to her from across the water. It was Joe Smithers, one of the fishermen. She waved and ran down to help him dock his boat.

"I hear you're leaving tomorrow," Joe said as he threw her the bowline. "Too bad. We always miss you when you go."

"Someday I just won't go," Belinda said. A gull who was eating some scraps from Joe's catch suddenly put up his head and screamed a complaint. "Oh, hush," Belinda said grumpily. She took the two empty baskets Joe handed her and stacked them on the dock.

"Bad catch today," Joe muttered. "Fish have gone deep."

"Why are the boats all coming in early?" Belinda asked. "We saw them from Granny May's porch."

"Got to," Joe said. "There's a big storm coming. They say it will hit sometime tomorrow afternoon, but it looks to me like it might be earlier than that. Worst one since '38. That's what the radio is saying."

"Tomorrow?" Belinda cried. "I'm supposed to go home tomorrow."

Joe winked. "Well, maybe this is the year you'll stay with us. I doubt Captain Jack will run the ferry in a hurricane."

"Really?" Belinda asked. She looked up at the sky. It was still clear, but she could see some big clouds building up over the mainland. "Funny, I've been so busy today I haven't even noticed the weather." She patted her pocket, feeling the comforting bulge of her wallet. "I'd better run. I've got a couple more errands to do. We're celebrating Granny May's birthday tonight," Belinda said.

Belinda ran up the hill and down the main street of town. In the grocery store, everybody was talking about the hurricane.

"Is it true the ferry won't run?" Belinda asked Mrs. Watson when she paid for the fudge sauce.

"I can't tell you for sure, honey. All I know is Captain Jack told Mr. Watson to meet him down by the dock first thing in the morning so they can batten the boat down till this thing blows over. Radio's talking about evacuating some of the towns on the mainland. We're okay out here. This island's got some high spots. We'll ride it out just the way we did in '38.''

Belinda's next stop was Miss Lizzie's gift shop, two doors down. She opened the door carefully and stepped inside. Nobody was in the store. Belinda reached up and stopped the jangling bells. She wanted to be alone for a moment just to enjoy this, but Miss Lizzie had already come out from the back of the store. "Belinda, how long have you been here? I was in the back listening to the radio. I guess I didn't hear the bell. This hurricane talk has driven everything else out of my head." Suddenly, Miss Lizzie put her hand up to her mouth. "Oh Belinda, you've come for the necklace."

But Belinda was already at the glass counter searching for it.

"It's not here," Belinda cried. "Miss Lizzie, what happened to it?"

"Oh honey, you hadn't been back in here for a while, and I thought maybe you'd decided on something else. A lady came yesterday and bought it for her daughter."

"But I finally saved all the money," Belinda said. "The whole fifteen dollars. It took me all month."

"Oh, I feel just terrible. There must be something else here that Granny May would like," Miss Lizzie said desperately. "Look at these nice pot holders that Anne Smithers brought in."

Belinda shook her head. She had her heart set on that necklace, and now nothing else would do.

"Miss Lizzie, who made the necklace?" Belinda asked. "I could go to her and buy a different one. She must have some others."

Miss Lizzie looked even more unhappy. "I can't tell you, Belinda. That's the trouble. I promised I would never tell anybody who the jeweler is. He wants it kept a secret."

Belinda stuffed her wallet into the back pocket of her shorts. A secret was a secret. She wouldn't try to pry it out of Miss Lizzie. That wasn't fair. But she had found out one thing: A man had made the necklace.

"Thanks Miss Lizzie. Good-bye."

"Oh Belinda, I am so sorry."

Outside, the sky had turned grayer and the wind had come up a bit, but Belinda didn't pay much attention. She was thinking too hard.

"Could it be Mr. Smithers?" she asked herself. "No. I've been to his house. I would have seen the shells or the gold. Maybe Mr. Marcus, the teacher. He goes off island all summer. Who could it possibly be? I've got to figure it out tonight. Before I leave."

Battening Down

Belinda walked back up the main street of town. Some of the stores had closed early for the day.

A loud horn made her look up. It was Joe and one of his friends in his pickup truck.

"Belinda, we're going up to your place to help Granny May tie down her boat. Want a ride?"

"No thanks, Joe. I'll walk. I'm trying to figure something out."

Joe glanced at the sky. "Don't take too long. Radio says the storm won't start until tomorrow, but it's looking kind of roiled up already."

He drove off with a wave.

"The hurricane," Belinda said. "Why, if there's a real hurricane, I bet I won't get off this island for a couple of days. That would give me the time I need. The island is so small. I know I could figure out who made that necklace by then."

All the way home, Belinda whispered her wish over and over. "Please let there be a hurricane. Please. Just enough of a hurricane to keep me here. I just need a little more time."

When she got home, the two men were rolling Granny May's yellow rowboat up over the lawn on old dock posts.

"Belinda, I was beginning to worry about you," Granny May said. "Have you heard about the hurricane?"

"Is it really coming?" Belinda asked.

"It looks that way," Granny May said.

"Belinda, can you hang on to the bow of this boat with Al?" Joe called. "I've got to move the back roller forward again."

Belinda ran to help. "Does the boat really have to come all the way up here under the porch?" she asked. "The water might rise that far?"

Joe glanced at the other man. "This may not be far enough, but it's all we've got time for. In '38, your grandmother's boat ended up on Mrs. Greenstone's front porch."

"But that's all the way across the road," Belinda cried in amazement.

"Honey, a hurricane is like a big dinosaur walking

around in your vegetable garden," said Al. "It doesn't care one single bit what it steps on."

Belinda wondered for a minute whether she could unwish her wish. A hurricane sounded like a powerful thing to fool around with.

Granny May came out on the porch. "I've found the candles and the matches, and a rope," she called down to Joe. "What else do I have to get together? It's been so long since we've had a big blow, I can't seem to remember."

"Well, you'd better get yourself some buckets, some flashlights, and the first aid kit, just in case. We'll be up to hammer the shutters closed in a little while."

"What about Ed Fletcher next door, Joe? He's going to need some help with that old motor boat of his," Granny May said.

"I'm going over to Fletcher's next," Joe said.

Belinda glanced over at Mr. Fletcher's house. She thought she saw someone peering at them through the curtain, but when she looked again the face was gone.

Dinner that night was not the celebration that Belinda had meant it to be. Belinda had no present to give her grandmother. They ate quickly because Granny May was busy cooking.

"Whenever I'm nervous, I cook," Granny May said with a little laugh. "It puts my mind on other things."

"What was the hurricane of '38 like?" Belinda asked.

Granny May wiped her hands on her apron and put a bowl of apples in front of Belinda. "Peel those for me, please, and slice them." She turned back to the stove where three pots were bubbling away.

"Your grandfather was alive then, of course, so we rode that one out together. The water came up over the seawall, up the lawn and over the porch. I remember we had towels stuffed under that door. Kind of silly really, trying to hold back all that water with a pile of bath towels, but then when you're in a hurricane you keep thinking you've seen the worst of it. Then right in the middle of all the crashing and howling and blowing, it suddenly stopped just as if somebody turned the faucet off. That's when the eye was passing over."

"What's the eye?" Belinda asked.

"The eye is the very center of the storm, just like the hole in a doughnut. You step outside into this eerie still world with the wreckage of the storm all about you. The air feels very heavy. They say that the frigate birds travel all the way up here from the Caribbean Ocean in the eye of a hurricane. They get caught in there, and they can't get out, so they just stay until the storm blows itself out over the Atlantic." Granny May's eyes were shining. In the silence, the wind blew a shutter against the house. "Joe must have missed that one. We'll have to hammer it tight in the morning," Granny May said as she turned back to the stove.

"But the storm starts up again after the eye?" Belinda asked.

"That's right. And it can be just as wicked and just as wild."

Belinda shivered. Neither one of them said anything for a moment. In the silence, there came a loud knocking at the door.

A Visitor

"Whoever could that be at this hour?" asked Granny
May. "Go and see, will you, Belinda?"

Belinda didn't really want to go. After Granny May's
story, she could almost believe it was the hurricane
knocking at their front door. The wind had already
begun to press against the house, and she was scared it
might suck her right out into the night.

To her amazement, it was Mr. Fletcher. She peered
around to be sure Fishface wasn't there before she
stepped aside to let him in.

"Hullo," he said gruffly, turning his hat round and
round in his hands. "Is your grandmother here?"

"Yes. She's in the kitchen."

"Why, hello Ed," said Granny May, pushing the wispy pieces of her hair up off her forehead.

"Cooking something, I see," he said as he let himself carefully down the three steps to the kitchen. For the first time, Belinda noticed that Mr. Fletcher had a limp. She realized she had never even seen him outside his house before.

Granny May laughed. "Oh Ed, you know I always cook when I'm nervous."

Mr. Fletcher nodded.

Belinda stood looking at the two of them. She couldn't imagine her cheerful Granny May even speaking to Mr. Fletcher, but after all, she thought, they had lived side by side for years.

"I came about the storm," Mr. Fletcher said. "Joe Smithers told me about your invitation. That's awful nice of you, May, but I don't think I better come over here." He glanced at Belinda, and she grew uncomfortable under his gaze. "They say it's going to be a bad one this time around. I expect we're due for it. But the dog and me, you know, we've been through a lot of things together. We're kind of used to being on our own." His voice ran out like a toy that has wound down.

"I should have told Joe that was an order, not an invitation. Don't be so ridiculous, Ed. Your house is much closer to the shore than ours. The water will be in your living room in no time if this storm is half as bad as they say it's going to be. Then what will you do with your bad leg and the dog to worry about?" Granny May asked. "If you come over here, Belinda and I will stay out of your way."

Mr. Fletcher looked like a little boy who'd been caught stealing. He shifted nervously from one foot to the other. Belinda smiled to herself, horrified as she was by this whole plan. When Granny May put her mind to something, nobody could change it.

"Well, I expect you're right, May," said Mr. Fletcher as he started to back out the door. He looked at Belinda again. "I'll keep the dog tied up," he muttered before he ducked under the kitchen door frame and limped off across the lawn.

"Granny May, couldn't Mr. Fletcher go across the street to Mrs. Greenstone's? I mean, it's probably even safer over there," Belinda said quickly.

"Belinda! You have to think of your neighbors at a time like this," Granny May said. "You know it was very hard for Ed to say yes to our invitation. I expect it was that dog that made up his mind in the end."

"I wanted to be all alone with you during the storm," Belinda said. She didn't say, "And I think Mr. Ed Fletcher is a mean old man with a mean old dog," but it seemed that Granny May knew what Belinda was thinking even when Belinda didn't want her to know.

"Ed Fletcher is a not a simple man, Belinda."

"Was he ever married?" Belinda asked.

"Yes. As I understand it, the only time Ed's been off

this island was in 1918 when he went to fight the Germans in the First World War. To everybody's amazement, he came back with a wife, an American nurse he met in Paris. I met her once when we first came on the island in 1923. She was very talkative, eager to make friends."

"The complete opposite of him," Belinda said.

"Opposites attract," Granny May said as she pulled a pie out of the oven. "But in this case, it didn't work. I think the loneliness of the island just drove her crazy. She ran off and left him one day, and she never came back. Ed went after her. He never told anybody whether he found her or not, but when he came back, she didn't come with him. After that, he kept to himself."

"Maybe he thinks people are still talking about it," Belinda said.

"Maybe," Granny May replied. "And maybe it's not that simple."

"I still wish it were just going to be the two of us," Belinda said.

Granny May came around and gave her a hug. "Remember, Belinda, there are good things inside everyone, even Ed Fletcher. This time together will give you a chance to go looking for them."

"Go looking for them," Belinda muttered as she climbed the stairs to bed. "I'm going to stay as far away from those two as I can." She fell asleep to the sound of the bell buoy clanging insistently in the rising wind and the faint growling of Fishface under the porch next door.

The Hurricane Begins

When Belinda woke up the next morning, she missed the noisy screeching of the gulls and the warm sunlight on her face. Outside, the sky looked dark and stirred up. Everything that could blow in the wind was blowing, from the halyards on the few boats still in the harbor to Granny May's loose shutter.

Belinda dressed quickly and ran downstairs. Granny May was up and already listening to the radio. The bittersweet smell of coffee filled the kitchen.

"It's really coming, isn't it?" Belinda asked, kissing Granny May on the top of her head as she passed. "The sky looks so dark, and the gulls are all hiding away somewhere. I feel scared and excited all at the same time."

"That's the right way to feel," Granny May said. "The

storm passed over New Haven and New York early this morning. Listen." She nodded at the radio.

"At five o'clock this morning, the winds at the center of the storm were clocked at 95 miles an hour. They are expected to decrease in velocity somewhat as long as the storm remains over land. At this time, the National Weather Service estimates that the storm will continue in a northeasterly direction at approximately 40 miles per hour. The full fury of the hurricane is expected to hit the Maine coast in the middle of the afternoon. And now, we have a report from John Davis on the cleanup operation in New Haven."

"Turn it off," Granny May said.

Belinda flipped the knob. It was a relief to have that grim voice shut off.

"We certainly don't need to hear what's happened to New Haven, since there's nothing we can do about it," Granny May said. "I spoke to your father this morning. He had heard the radio reports and wanted to make sure we were all battened down. He says to tell you that you are very lucky. He never did go through a hurricane on the island, and he always wanted to."

"What about them?" Belinda asked. "Will the hurricane hit them?"

"No, it passed to the east of them. All right now, let's worry about more important things, such as breakfast. I vote for scrambled eggs, bacon, fresh orange juice, muffins, and our very own blueberry jam. We'll make it a special hurricane feast."

Belinda nodded. She didn't feel much like eating, but she couldn't dampen Granny May's enthusiasm. "Are we going to be all right, Granny May?" she asked.

"It will be a little scary, Belinda, no doubt about it. The storm's turned out to be bigger than anyone predicted." Granny May came over and gave her a quick hug. "But this little house has been through some rougher weather than this and survived it. Don't worry too much."

The wind continued to rise, and the rain started soon after they had cleared away the breakfast dishes. The two of them put on their slickers and went out on the porch to secure the loose shutter. They had to shout at one another over the growing noise of the storm. Belinda could barely see the town dock through the deepening fog and the rain. The tide was running into the harbor, chased by the wind, so the bigger swells were already crashing up over the seawall.

Just then, Ed Fletcher parted the hedge and stumped across the lawn, carrying a flat black suitcase and Fish-face's bed. His head was bent down against the rain, and the sides of his poncho billowed out with each gust of wind.

"He looks like a big yellow balloon," Belinda shouted into her grandmother's ear.

Mr. Fletcher turned once and made some noise that Belinda couldn't hear. In response to it, Fishface pushed his own way through the lower part of the hedge and trotted after the man.

"They even look alike," Belinda said out loud, knowing nobody could hear her.

Granny May motioned them all inside. There was no use trying to talk out on the porch.

"Water's already halfway up my porch steps," Mr. Fletcher said.

"Don't think we'll go out again till it's blown over," Granny May said cheerily. They all lifted off their wet slickers and hung them on the pegs by the door. "Ed, why don't you just take over the dining room and make that your place while you're here. There's a bathroom through that far door, and you can close both of the other doors if you need some privacy."

While Granny May was talking, Fishface was prowling along the edges of the room snuffling to himself. Belinda stood very still, hoping he would not recognize her as the lawn mower pusher, invader of his territory. He stopped when he got to her rubber boot and looked up. Belinda smiled hopefully. Fishface bared his teeth and growled.

Mr. Fletcher whistled. "Doesn't like being cooped up. Never has," he said. "I had to leave him out all last night. He slept under the porch."

"I heard him growling," Belinda said. "It sounded as if he wanted to have a good fight with a hurricane."

Mr. Fletcher took Fishface into the dining room with him and closed the door.

"Oh dear," Belinda said. "This is going to be a long day."

Lights Out

Belinda and Granny May built a fire, which took a long time to catch because of the rain coming down the chimney. Mr. Fletcher did not come out of the dining room. Belinda could hear him moving around in there.

"It sounds as if he's rearranging the furniture," Belinda muttered. Granny May lifted her eyebrows as if to say, "It's none of our business." She went back into the kitchen to fill up the ice chest in case the electricity went off.

Belinda wandered around the house. She thought it was going to be bad to have Mr. Fletcher with them, but it was worse than she had even imagined.

"How can I get to know him if he won't come out of the dining room?" she asked her grandmother.

29

Granny May laughed. "You'd better find something to do, Belinda. Waiting out hurricanes has been known to drive people crazy. It's like waiting for the water to boil on the stove."

Belinda went upstairs to the shell chest and picked out her ten favorite scallop shells. With this hurricane, she would never be able to find out who the jeweler was, but maybe she could try to make a necklace herself. She set herself up at the card table in the corner of the living room with an ice pick, a hammer, some fishing line, and a box of Magic Markers.

"Granny May, don't come in the living room, please. I'm doing something secret."

"All right," Granny May called from the kitchen.

Belinda had broken four of the first five shells trying to make holes in them with the ice pick, when she felt somebody in the room with her.

Mr. Fletcher was standing at the window, staring out at the storm.

"I didn't hear you come in," Belinda said. She knew it sounded rude, but she was in a bad mood over the broken shells.

"Water's up over the seawall already," he said, as much to himself as to her.

Belinda didn't answer. The shell project had distracted her from the hurricane. He came and stood behind her.

"The scallops break easily," he said.

"You can say that again," she replied. "If this keeps up, I won't have any left."

"Too bad," he said, turning away. "Ice pick's too big. You got a needle in the house?"

"Would you help me?" asked Belinda, surprised.

He frowned. "I don't know. I'm not too good with my hands." But after a moment's hesitation, he pulled up a chair and sat down beside her. "You'd better bring me some more shells."

She ran to get him a needle from the sewing box, half expecting to find he had left when she returned.

"I'm not promising I won't break them," he said.

"It's all right. I have a whole drawerful upstairs. I collected them all summer."

"Where do you find them?" he asked.

"Granny May and I have a secret place down on South Beach. There's one big rock that's been washed away by the waves, so it curls around like a U. The shells get caught in there when the tide goes down."

He didn't answer.

She bent her head over the Magic Markers, glancing at him from time to time out of the corner of her eye. For someone who wasn't very good with his hands, he seemed to be doing pretty well. He had only broken one shell so far, and he was on the second to last when the electricity went out.

"You know where the candles are?" he asked without looking up from his work.

She jumped up and brought him one from the supply in the dining room sideboard. Fishface growled half-heartedly at her from his place under the table, but for once he seemed to realize that she wasn't the real enemy.

He lit the candle and waved her away. "Better make sure your grandmother doesn't need any help," he said.

Granny May was busy shifting the food from the freezer to the ice chest.

"We'll leave the things in the refrigerator for a while. It will hold the cold as long as we don't open the door too often. Now, what have you been up to in the living room?" she asked.

"Secrets," said Belinda.

Mr. Fletcher had finished nine shells and was back at the window.

"Thank you," Belinda said. "I would have gone through my whole drawer before I had ten good ones."

He didn't answer.

"I'm making a necklace for Granny May," she said, lowering her voice. "I had one all picked out at Miss Lizzie's, but a lady bought it yesterday."

"Belinda, can I come in now?" Granny May called.

"All right, but walk slowly," Belinda called back. She blew out the candle and draped her damp slicker over the table.

Granny May joined Mr. Fletcher at the window.

"Water's whipping up," he said. "It's already over the wall."

Belinda had been so caught up with Mr. Fletcher and the necklace, she had completely forgotten the storm. Standing there in the dim room, she became aware of a steady moaning that sounded like Fishface in distress.

"What is that noise?" she asked, peering through the window.

"That's the wind. I remember that noise from the last bad storm," Granny May said. "It feels as if the storm has wrapped its arms around the house and is trying to squeeze us to death."

The wind was driving the rain at the house like a hose turned on full blast, and some of the windows had begun to leak from the force of the water. There were moments of clearing outside when Belinda could see beyond the porch railing. She was reminded of the sand walls she liked to build on the beach when the tide was rising. Eventually, a wave would wash over them, and when the water rushed back to the sea, there would be nothing left of her wall but a sodden lump of sand. For the first time, Belinda was really scared. She went and stood beside Granny May.

Granny May put her arm around Belinda's shoulders. "You come with me and help me find those flashlights. Then we'll start eating some of that food in the refrigerator."

The Waters Rise

They were sitting around the kitchen table, eating blueberry pie by the light of two candles, when Fishface began to howl. He had been pacing back and forth in the dining room, making strange noises and pawing at the rug for quite a while.

"It's the pressure falling as we get near the eye," Mr. Fletcher said. "Dogs can feel the change even more than humans. It makes him nervous."

The howling was awful. It said out loud all the fears that the people in the house were keeping inside.

Mr. Fletcher tried first to comfort the dog, and when that didn't work, he shouted at him.

"Fishface, quiet."

The howling subsided for a moment, but as soon as Mr. Fletcher left the dining room, it started again.

"Bring him in here, Ed," said Granny May. "I wouldn't want to be left all alone at a time like this either."

But Fishface began to go even crazier when Mr. Fletcher let him off the leash. He threw himself at the back door, whining and scratching. When they didn't open the door, he put up his head and howled again.

"I can't stand this," Mr. Fletcher muttered. "I'm going to take him out for just a minute. Maybe if he sees what's out there, he'll realize how lucky he is to be inside with us."

Belinda jumped up. "I've got the flashlight," she said quickly. "I'll get your slicker from the living room." Fishface was making her so nervous, she couldn't sit in the same room with him any longer.

The moment she got into the living room, she knew something was wrong. There was an ominous sound of splashing water. Her flashlight picked up the puddle coming in under the front door. It seemed to double in size as she stood there and stared. She grabbed their slickers and the ten perfect shells off the card table and ran back into the kitchen.

"Granny May," she cried. "The water's coming in under the porch door."

"Holy Moses," Granny May said. "Now we're in for

it. Go upstairs and throw down all the towels you can find. Hurry, Belinda. Ed, you'd better stay right here. If the water's up over the porch, it must have filled up the back yard by now."

But he didn't answer. He unlocked the back door and yanked it open against the pull of the wind. The storm burst into the kitchen like a wild uninvited guest, knocking over the vase on the table and blowing out the candles. Bending down against the rain, Mr. Fletcher pushed out the screen door, dragging a terrified Fishface behind him. Then the doors slammed, and Belinda and Granny May were alone for a moment.

"Heavens," said Granny May. "I'd like to take this hurricane over my knee and spank it. What a lot of noise and trouble it's making."

Despite herself, Belinda had to smile at the picture of Granny May spanking the storm like a bad little boy. She ran upstairs to get the towels.

"Here they come," Belinda called as she leaned over the bannister and dropped one pile and then another, straight out of the linen closet.

"Never mind," Granny May yelled. "It's too late. Come down and we'll try to save some of what's in here."

They took off their shoes and sloshed around in the rising water, taking the pictures off the walls and the drawers out of Granny May's desk.

"Where is that Ed Fletcher now that we really need

him?" Granny May said as she piled another chair on the couch. "All right, abandon ship. Let's take some food upstairs."

"Shouldn't we go over to Mrs. Greenstone's house?" Belinda said.

"Too late now, Belinda. I'm afraid we'd have to swim over, and I don't think this old lady has the strength. Now where is Ed and that blasted dog?"

Just then the kitchen door blew open again, and Mr. Fletcher reappeared. He pushed the door shut behind him and leaned against it, breathing heavily.

"Ed, where's the dog?" Granny May said.

"He's gone," he said. "One minute he was there, and then the leash was yanked out of my hand and I didn't see him again. The water's coming up so fast. He was just swept away."

"I'm sure he'll be all right," Belinda said, touching Mr. Fletcher's wet sleeve. "I bet he was swept right over to Mrs. Greenstone's house. She'll take him in until the storm is over."

Mr. Fletcher put one hand over his eyes and began to cry. Granny May took his arm.

"Ed, we've got to get upstairs now. There's two feet of water in the living room, and it's begun to seep in here."

"My tools," he cried, suddenly. "I've got to get my tools."

39

He pulled away from the two of them and rushed into the dining room.

"What tools?" Belinda said, but Granny May did not answer. She was filling up a box with food.

"Take this upstairs, Belinda, and come down as quickly as you can for the next one."

The Eye of the Hurricane

They moved into the two bedrooms upstairs. Granny May lit the candles and set all the food in one corner on the bookshelves.

"There now," she said. "Just like home."

They both glanced at Mr. Fletcher, who had not said a word. He was sitting on the bed, staring out the window, one hand on his black briefcase. He looked so sad and lost that Belinda wanted to go up and hug him, but she didn't dare.

Every so often the house shook as a piece of floating debris crashed into it. The water was filled with all kinds of surprises: pieces of boats, mattresses, roofs of houses, furniture, clothing. On one of her trips to the bottom of the stairs to check the level of the water, Belinda saw a box of dolls floating by the window.

Late in the afternoon, in the middle of a game of gin rummy, Granny May said, "Listen, I hear the change. Here comes the hole in the doughnut."

Belinda put down her cards. The wind had subsided, and there was an eerie calm around the house. Belinda walked down the hall and looked out the back window. The yard had turned into a small pond, and she could just make out the door of the garage across the water. In one corner, where the fence connected to the wall of the garage, there was a pile of debris. She looked closer. Something was moving around on top of a table.

"Mr. Fletcher," she screamed. "Come here quickly. I see Fishface. He's alive. Hurry."

The two old people came racing down the hall.

"Where?" Mr. Fletcher said.

"There," Belinda said, pointing. "By the garage."

"I'm going to get him," Mr. Fletcher said.

"No you don't, Ed Fletcher. With that bum leg, you won't get beyond the back porch," Granny May said, grabbing the old man by the arm. "And if you were stranded out there, we couldn't save you. Fishface has done just fine up till now. He's in a protected spot. The storm will wear itself out soon."

"For God's sake, May, let me go."

While the two of them argued, Belinda turned back to

the window. Fishface was pacing around and around on the tabletop, as if trying to decide whether or not to jump.

"We can't leave him out there the whole time," Belinda cried. "I'll go."

She twisted away and ran down the stairs before Granny May could say no. The water in the kitchen was up to the seats of the chairs. The sight of it stopped her. Mr. Fletcher came down behind her. He was carrying a life preserver and a coil of rope.

"What's left of the wind is blowing in the right direction, towards the garage," he said as he put the life preserver over her head and fastened it. He tied the rope around her waist, leaving a few feet to dangle. "As soon as you get a hold of his collar, tie this end of the rope to it, and I'll pull you both back. Your granny will be watching from upstairs, and if she thinks you're having any trouble, she'll yell at me to pull you back."

For a moment, Belinda wished she had never offered.

"He doesn't like me, Mr. Fletcher," she said. "What if he tries to bite me?"

"Then leave him," Mr. Fletcher said without looking at her.

They pushed their way through the water in the kitchen. He opened the door, and she launched herself quickly before she had time to get scared. The water felt cold at first. The hardest thing was trying to swim with the heavy life preserver, but as Mr. Fletcher had said, the current and the wind blew her in the right direction. A plastic box brushed her shoulder and floated away.

Halfway across the back yard, she put her feet down and, to her surprise, she touched ground. Then she half swam, half walked to the corner. Fishface saw her and began to whimper, pacing back and forth on his tabletop. As she drew closer, the whining changed to a low growl.

"Now listen to me, you stupid dog, I'm not going to get near you if you start that," she shouted. "I came all the way out here to save you, and if you don't want to spend the rest of this hurricane out here, then you'd better just be quiet and listen." The tone of her voice shut him right up, so she kept on talking to him just that way as she pushed aside the garbage cans and the chair that were bumping up against his table. "I hope you know how to swim, Fishface, because if you don't, you're in big trouble." He let her tie the rope around his collar without a sound.

"All right," she yelled waving back at the house. "Let's go."

The rope tightened so quickly that it pulled her off her feet. Fishface skidded off his table and into the water with a splash. He soon recovered and was paddling up next to her, the rope slack between them. At one point, a large piece of wood came up between them and caught on the rope.

"Hold your breath," Belinda shouted as she pulled the rope down. The dog disappeared for a moment and came back up, spluttering, but free of the wood. After that, he seemed to get tired, because he paddled less energetically and slipped behind her.

The wind was rising again, and Belinda had a hard time keeping her head above the water and watching for obstacles at the same time. At last, she was back at the kitchen door, and Mr. Fletcher pulled them both inside with one enormous yank on the rope.

Granny May was waiting on the landing. "Well now," she said, folding Belinda into her arms. "Look what the storm swept in." When Belinda looked up, she saw tears in Granny May's eyes. Belinda began to cry too, now that she was safe inside. Mr. Fletcher put a towel around her and helped her upstairs to bed. She vaguely remembered Granny May changing her into her nightgown, and then she fell asleep.

Mr. Fletcher's Secret

When she woke up the next morning, the first thing Belinda heard was a sea gull sitting on the roof outside her window, screaming at the world.

She sat right up and peered out. It was still drizzling but, for the first time in two days, she could see right out across the harbor. It was a gray sea of floating objects that bobbed and bumped into one another.

And there was no wind. The hurricane was over.

"Granny May," she called out, suddenly afraid that the storm had swept them away while she slept.

"We're down here, floating around in the kitchen, Belinda," her grandmother called back.

She found Granny May and Mr. Fletcher, mopping the floor.

"Is Fishface all right?" she asked.

"Fine Belinda," Mr. Fletcher said with a smile. Belinda realized it was the first time he had ever said her name. "He's even better than you are at sleeping through the second half of a hurricane."

"Enough chattering, you two. We've got work to do," Granny May said. "First, Belinda has to eat some breakfast, and then we have to clean up the living room and head over to Ed's house. Joe just towed the yellow rowboat back. They found it up by the town dock."

"Was anybody hurt in the storm?" Belinda asked.

"No, not that we've heard about. Most of the people spent the night in the town hall, playing poker and having a high old time." Granny May snorted in mock disapproval.

Later on, when Granny May was deep in the refrigerator, fussing over the wasted food, Mr. Fletcher called Belinda into the dining room.

Fishface looked up and growled at her halfheartedly. "Oh be quiet, you silly dog," Belinda said with a laugh.

"I have something for you," Mr. Fletcher said. He was shifting back and forth from one foot to the other.

Before Belinda had even unwrapped the tissue paper, she knew what it was. The scallop shells were a little smaller, but other than that, this necklace was almost exactly the same as the one in the store.

"You're the jeweler!" she cried.

"Yes," he said. "Only a few people know—your grandmother and Miss Lizzie."

"But why do you keep it a secret?" Belinda asked. "If I could make something as beautiful as this, I would tell everybody about it."

"I've got my reasons," he said. "And my pride. I don't want people thinking I need the money."

"I can pay for it," she said. "That's why I was mowing your lawn. I was saving up to buy the necklace for Granny May." She stopped, realizing what she had said. "I'm sure you don't need the money, but I just want you to know I've got it. Pride, I guess," she added with a shrug.

He smiled. "It's a present," he said. "Or an exchange. You show me where you find the scallop shells down on South Beach. Maybe next year, we could go into business together. I'm getting too old to tramp around the island looking for shells."

She ran her fingers over the scallop shells, edged in gold.

"We'll give it to her together," Belinda said.

"Not right now," he said. "Maybe tomorrow."

They looked at each other for a moment without saying anything. Then he turned away and began to pack up the rest of his things.

"Wait," Belinda cried. "I have something for you." She came back downstairs with the ten perfect scallop shells. "You can make another necklace with these. If you don't mind the coloring."

"I don't mind," he said. His voice sounded gruff and distant, as if he had already slipped away from her again, back behind the window shades.

The ferry did not run for three days after the storm, because so much debris had to be cleared away from the entrance to the slip.

"Wonderful," cried Belinda when she heard the news. "Now we can really celebrate your birthday, Granny May. This time I have a present for you. And we can invite Mr. Fletcher."

Granny May laughed. "Mr. Fletcher," she cried. "That mean old man who lives next door with the vicious dog? You don't mean it."

"People are allowed to change their minds, Mrs. Edwards," said Belinda in a dignified voice.

But Mr. Fletcher would not come to the door when Belinda knocked. She was sure he was there, because Fishface was tied up under the porch as usual. She thought she saw the curtain move a little, but she couldn't be sure.

"I know he's in there," Belinda said to her grandmother as they were putting the dry rugs back down in the living room. "Why won't he answer me?"

Granny May sat down on her armchair with a bump. "That's hard work," she said, pushing her hair back off her head. "Belinda, remember the bank you found up in the attic at the beginning of your visit?"

"You mean the one with the hand that reaches out and grabs the penny? The one that used to be Daddy's?"

Granny May nodded. "Just think of Ed Fletcher as that hand. He popped out of his house, and he let you see an awful lot of him in the last few days, and I don't just mean his face. Seems to me he let you see inside of him, too. Well, now he's popped back inside again, and he's going to stay there for a while."

"But he's not mean the way he pretends to be," Belinda said.

"No, he's not mean on the inside. But it's hard for people to change their outsides overnight."

Belinda gave Granny May the necklace at dinner that night, just before the birthday cake.

Granny May opened the box very slowly, neatly folding the wrapping paper and coiling the ribbon before she pulled aside the tissue paper to look at her present.

"Hurry Granny May, you are torturing me," Belinda cried.

Granny May's smile of delight was worth a whole month of Fishface. "It is lovely," she said softly, running her finger around the gold edges. "Here Belinda, you'll have to hook it for me. My fingers don't work that well anymore."

"Oh, it looks wonderful on you," Belinda said. "Just

the way I thought it would. That's why I wished for the hurricane. I figured with a little more time I could find another necklace like the one I saw for you at Miss Lizzie's. But I didn't mean the hurricane to be quite so big and quite so badly behaved," Belinda added with a grin.

"Next time you're wishing for something, Miss Edwards, I wish you'd give me some warning," Granny May said. "So Ed told you his secret?"

"Yes. You know, he said I could be his partner next summer. He wants me to collect the shells," Belinda said.

"You'd have to keep his secret," Granny May warned.

"Oh, I know that," Belinda said.

"It'll be a strange partnership all right. You're such different people, Belinda. One so private and the other so open."

"Opposites attract," replied Belinda with a smile.